I0579039

Home Before Dark

A Stella Madison Caper

Lilly Maytree

LIGHTSMITH PUBLISHERS

Thorne Bay, Alaska

Copyright © 2021 Lilly Maytree

All rights reserved.

ISBN: 978-1-944798-41-3

No part of this book may be reproduced or transmitted in any form or by any means electronic or mechanical, including photocopying, recording, or by any information storage and retrieval system, without the written permission of the publisher.

Published in the United States by

Lightsmith Publishers
P.O. Box 19293
Thorne Bay, Alaska 99919

Website: www.LightsmithPublishers.com

Cover photography by Steve and Becky Brown

Lightsmith Publishers is an imprint of the Wilderness School Institute, a non-profit educational organization that offers outdoor youth activities in wilderness settings, including training in wilderness skills and nature studies, as well as the publication of curriculum on related subjects, through the Wilderness School Press, and their children's imprint Summers Island Press.

Home Before Dark / Lightsmith Publishers Edition / Paperback

To all those who struggle with life's changes...may you never be alone.

"Many have puzzled themselves about the origin of evil. I am content to observe that there is evil, and that there is a way to escape from it..."

John Newton.

1

When opportunity first knocked on Stella Madison's door, she thought it was the devil. Had to be. That's because an unexpected change in circumstances was the last thing a person in her situation would look for. But there it was. Glaring up at her from the letter she had just opened to read with her second cup of morning coffee. "Dear Ms. Madison, we regret to inform you that the building in which you are living..."

But why go into all that. It wasn't the real problem, anyway. The real problem— not counting the emotional stress and strain of moving at her age (a women in her sixties!)—was the fact that she hadn't a penny beyond her monthly expenses to do it with. She lived on a fixed income. And even though she had always kept current with her driver's license, she didn't own a vehicle. Hadn't driven herself anywhere in years. It made her wonder how she would go about even looking for a new place, much less move all of her things into one.

Stella had a lot of things.

To be perfectly honest, she had accumulated about twice as many things as she originally came with, ten years ago. Any way you looked at it, she was in a pickle, and with only thirty days to get out of it. Thirty days! Could big companies really do that to people? Well, they could. So, obviously, she needed a plan.

After having lived in her own familiar world of comfort and safety for so long, the thought of taking a job was appalling. But desperate times called for desperate measures. She could endure anything for a short time, and this situation was only temporary. All right, so she had vowed never to set foot in that crazy rat-race of a working world, again. Things were upside down out there! Not to mention the natural disasters, where people like her were not only overlooked, but got trampled.

Which is why Stella had made it her priority not to depend on anyone but herself.

And, the thought of having to answer to somebody (probably half her age) after having grown so independent, was about the most distasteful thing she could think of. But she would just have to get a grip on herself and buck up. The trouble was, it had been over ten years since Stella had "worked" at anything.

What on earth could she do?

She had always been good with children...only she didn't have the strength and energy to meet the demands of kids these days. Not to mention it was now illegal to discipline any of them. Working at the local coffee shop was out, too, as she had never been fast enough with numbers and cash machines to keep people happy. Selling something was not an option. The only things she had that would be of the slightest value to anyone else were books. Stella loved books and had spent the greater portion of her life collecting for a personal library that now numbered in the thousands.

There were not only bookcases in every room of her small, one bedroom apartment that overlooked the sea (well, it was only tiny sliver of sea, actually, that disappeared entirely when the fog was in), but also shelves that ran throughout the apartment, about a foot below the ceiling. All categorized by the Dewy Decimal System.

Which suddenly gave her an idea.

She could work at the county library. It was within walking distance, and she was as familiar with it as her own kitchen. What's more, it was quiet... which meant a lot to her. She even knew some of the staff.

Which— as it turned out—was the only reason she was able to land any kind of a job there at all. Never mind that she had once been a schoolteacher, or that she loved to read. According to Ester Fergeson, who spoke up for her, the Clerk I positions were the only ones that ever came open anymore. Unless someone above that either died or retired. A Clerk I position was a person who restocked shelves. For an extremely minimum wage.

So it was that Stella Madison, with her lively blue eyes and striking white hair that tucked neatly under, began working five and a half hours a day at the Whitcomb Ritter Library. Four days a week, three days before the end of the next pay period. It wasn't until after she had been formally hired that she found out Clerk I people were only allowed part-time. Something about benefits. To be honest, Stella would have been hard-pressed to put in a full day at any job. Considering her situation. And the fact that it was imperative that she be home before dark. (Her number one rule for staying safe was that she always got home before dark. Safety was something a woman alone had to be constantly aware of. There were desperate people who prowled around in the city after dark.)

Her love of books carried her through. Which was a good thing, because according to her calculations, it seemed hardly possible to pay off the cost of this moving thing before her hundredth birthday. A thought that made her wonder if the entire experience wasn't making her rather cynical...an attitude that eventually led to trouble.

The truth is, Stella had problems from the very first day.

Not with any of the procedures. She knew that Dewey Decimal System like the back of her hand. Not with the computers, either: she had been using one of her own for years, now. It made her feel like something of a world traveler to exchange emails with friends on other continents.

She was even rather proud of her social abilities. Which is why it came as something of a shock to discover she couldn't "get along" very well with the rest of the staff. By the end of the first week, she was sure they were all morons. Including her friend, Ester.

Stella's first confrontation with a staff member happened on her very first day, in what later came to be known as "the egg incident."

"Is there a problem?" The senior librarian and supervisor of the shift looked away from her computer screen and peered over the rims of her reading glasses. She was a tall imposing woman, well dressed in a forest-colored business suit and black turtle-neck sweater. Her dark hair was twisted up neatly in one of those fashionable clips Stella admired but had never been able to get the hang of.

"Well, yes, Ms. Thatcher, there is." Stella stepped into the office and placed a book with a green, nondescript cover on the desk. "While I was re- shelving the six hundreds—the cooking section, that is—I found this copy of *The Egg And I* by Betty MacDonald."

"And where else should a book about eggs be, if not in the cooking section?"

For a split second Stella's blue eyes widened with surprise before she assumed the woman had simply been too caught up in what she was doing to hear her right. "You see that's the point. I happen to own a copy of this book, myself, and it has nothing to do with cooking. It's about a woman who married a chicken rancher and the miserable years they went through before their divorce. There isn't a recipe in the whole thing."

There were a few moments of awkward silence between them before Ms. Thatcher broke off eye- contact and busied herself thumbing through the pages a few moments. "Obviously a computer glitch," she finally pronounced. "The computers do all the cataloguing these days, and it's strictly by word association. But I see this was published way back in the forties... hasn't been checked out since 1989. Still has the signature slip we used before we automated." She closed the cover with a decisive thump, "Should have been turned over to FL years ago. Thank you, Stella. I'll take care of it."

"What is FL?"

"Friends of the Library. A nationwide organization that handles the sale of all our discards."

"Discards!" Stella gasped (she couldn't help it).

"But this was a beautifully written book —a bestseller. They even made a movie out of it starring Fred MacMurry and Claudette Colbert!"

"That may be. But it's a new age, isn't it, and this is hopelessly out-dated. I assure you our shelves are loaded down with a more than adequate supply of information on divorce. Or even chicken ranches for that matter. With all the latest and up-to-date information from around the world."

Around the world. Stella felt something like a balloon that was slowly losing its air, and stared for a few moments at the tips of her sensible leather slip-ons that were peeking out from under her gray wool slacks. What about all the worlds that no longer existed anymore? How did one go about traveling to them? Suppose a person wanted to "time travel" to experience a different age altogether? See what it was like back then. Maybe even pick up some useful bit of information that is no longer common knowledge these days. And how else was one supposed to become intimately acquainted with great minds if librarians could lop off the connection to the very works where they lived? Why that —Stella shuddered—was practically murder!

No wonder the young minds of today weren't interested in such things anymore. These lovely things were no longer a part of their life experience. Not by their own choice, as some would have us believe, but by the choice of some (some senior librarian!) who had made the choice for them. Now the children of the future must evolve out of the narrow-minded channels of a single generation instead of having the freedom to tap into the wisdom of the ages, right from their own neighborhoods.

"Outrageous!" Stella's indignation at the very thought of children being denied this ecstasy boiled over while she backed out of the office. As if Ms. Thatcher had suddenly revealed herself as a snake. "I'm going to—to formally complain to the authorities!"

Slamming the door on the way out was an accident.

The next confrontation occurred three days after that and was referred to (in the subsequent deposition) as "the coffee altercation." If it could be said that an incident was something one did, while an altercation was something one did to someone else, Stella should have realized by the very nature of these events that things were escalating.

Only she didn't.

2

It happened when she decided to approach Whitcomb Ritter Library's resident author. The term was casual, in the sense that everyone knew he didn't actually live at the facility: he could merely be found working there five days a week. Always in the same corner of the glass-enclosed study area where people could plug in their own laptop computers. If there was anyone who would object to this new policy that the majority of books in public libraries should be five years old or less, it would surely be somebody who wrote books.

It was commonly known that Colonel Oliver P. Henry was working on some sort of military history that—according to Stella—automatically made him a man of principle. He was a large man, broad enough about the middle to have to wear his shirts out rather than tucked in. He had wavy gray hair and a tan that one was apt to see on the younger athletic types rather than retirees. As if he must spend a lot of time at the beach.

He always took up the entire end of the same table, with his papers and things spread all over. That day he was wearing khaki pants and a multi-colored Hawaiian shirt that reminded Stella of the waiters down at the Luau Palace, where she ate occasionally on Sunday afternoons.

"Colonel Henry?" She whispered tentatively, though they were the only two people in the room. "May I bother you for a moment?"

"Yes, what is it," he whispered back and clicked the save button before glancing up at her, clearly trying to calculate if he was supposed to know her or not.

"We've never met," she replied to the questioning gaze. "My name is Stella Madison, and I was just wondering if—as a fellow book lover—you were aware of this new library policy to discard all the vintage books."

Once, again, it was as if she had interrupted someone's private world, and the Colonel had to blink twice before any semblance of thought replaced his blank stare. "Matter of logistics, I'd say. The place would have to be ten times the size if it didn't have some kind of rotation system. Other than the basics."

"What I'm trying to tell you, Colonel, is that there are no more basics."

Another brief silence as he thought about this. "They wouldn't dump the classics."

"They do maintain a small collection of those— I've just come from looking them up. But they have to meet very strict guidelines to be included. They have to be... what was the phrase Ms. Thatcher used... oh, yes—to be politically correct."

"My dear woman," the words were more exasperation than compliment, "nothing in this world changes more frequently than politics. But I hardly see what all this—"

"My point exactly." Stella moved closer and looked so intently into his green eyes that he shifted uncomfortably in his seat. "Don't you agree, Colonel Henry, that if we start changing our basics as quickly as we change our politics, society will soon be going in circles instead of moving forward?"

"Do you..." he drummed impatient fingers on the table, "have some sort of a petition you would like me to sign? Is that it?"

"Well, if you think it would help. What exactly should it say?"

"How should I know what it should say? I have a hard enough time deciding what I should say about things I do know something about. Now, if you'll excuse me,

I have work to do."

"What would you say..." Stella persisted. "If I told you there isn't a single copy of *Huckleberry Finn* in this entire library?"

"Considering the way people feel about racial slurs these days..." He returned his attention to the screen, then, as if the conversation were over. "I'd say it was good riddance."

"Obviously..." Stella was beginning to feel somewhat impatient herself. "You have never personally read it. *Huckleberry Finn* is a plea for us to be less bigoted in this world—not the other way around."

"Whatever it is a plea for, it doesn't concern me."

"Spoken like every other pompous, self-centered citizen who thinks the world owes you something and not that other way round!" Stella smacked the facing lid of his briefcase closed, and turned smartly to leave.

How was she supposed to know he had

a hot cup of coffee sitting in there?

She might have been let go for that. An employee had no business insulting patrons, much less getting physical. But—as everyone knew—it was against library policy to bring food or drinks inside. Beyond a minor yelp and leap to his feet to save the papers beneath, there wasn't much the Colonel could do about it. Especially after Stella went so far as to smuggle a stack of paper towels in from the ladies' room to help him clean up. If not for the fact that the walls were glass and they had a fairly large crowd that day, no one would have even noticed.

At any rate, she took over immediately. In fact, while the Colonel was at something of a loss to decide whether he should betray himself further by dumping the brand-name cup and wet napkins into the nearest waste-basket just outside the door, she whisked them away herself, along with an armload of splattered newspapers he had been going over. She took those over to a corner table where she quickly but discretely began wiping them off, then shaking them closed by each long wooden holder. The picture of efficiency until the last one. And as the Colonel was still recovering his balance from the unpleasant incident, he couldn't help staring at her through the glass.

The last two pages of that edition were stuck together with a sticky wetness that called for more than a brisk swipe. Stella pulled them gently apart and gasped at the picture of a youthful face smiling up at her. The headline read, "Matt Johnson Comes Home Today." Under that, it said, "Passengers on flight 342 waited respectfully as the casket bearing the remains of the young hero were accompanied by a uniformed escort toward waiting family members on the tarmac of the county airport. Johnson was a..."

Stella put a hand over her heart and closed her eyes for a few seconds of utter remorse. How much longer would it all go on? She couldn't bear to read anymore. Instead, she dabbed gently at the remaining drops, and carried the papers slowly to the media center, where she replaced them reverently back into the newspaper rack. Completely forgetting to apologize to the Colonel. Something she didn't realize until she was home sitting in her pajamas that night.

Linked with that brief pang of regret she always felt when confronted with such losses (Stella was an avid watcher of the nightly news), the coffee altercation became an even more disappointing experience. One that left her rather blue for the rest of the week. Not so much at the Colonel's lack of sympathy for future generations, but at her own embarrassing response to it. One could blame it on age or the financial strain she was under, but even Stella thought she had higher standards than that.

When, on the following Friday, she received another unexpected letter in the mail, stating that her building owners were going to pay each tenant a small moving reimbursement (maybe even enough to hire a moving van!), her troubles should have been partly relieved.

Except she hadn't found a half-decent place to move into, yet. Even though her circle of apartment- hunting around her own familiar neighborhood had widened to nearly a mile. They were all so expensive! Normally, that would have been enough to send her into a whole new fervor of anxiety. Only by then...something had mysteriously changed inside her.

Not only was she certain a place would show up if she kept looking, moving was not the most important thing on her mind any more. How could it be, when she was personally standing on the brink of what was a disastrous change in society and no one else seemed to care? Had everyone been brainwashed?

It wasn't until the following Tuesday that the rare opportunity revealed itself.

3

Never in her life had Stella considered herself an immoral person. Things like lying, cheating, and stealing were hardly in her vocabulary, much less, a part of her normal behavior. Which is why it came as an absolute shock to be accused of a crime. Crimes were things a degenerate few stayed awake nights plotting, or at least the result of an explosion of heated passions. Stella hadn't any forethought at all when she committed hers: it had simply been a reaction. Rather like an unexpected belch in public, or the need to blow one's nose.

In the beginning, she didn't feel as if

she were doing anything wrong. She felt like she was helping people. Which should have been warning enough if only she had been in her right mind. In her right mind, Stella knew better than anyone that "two wrongs never make right." Besides that, these new sins started out so small.

They started when she was assigned to work on the discards. They were stored in a room behind Ms. Thatcher's office and Stella was to remove each from the library data system and hand-stamp the word DISCARD inside each cover. Stacks and stacks of books. Nearly a thousand of them! It practically broke Stella's heart. Not simply because they would no longer be available to the general public, but because that horrible stamp would devalue the books in the eyes of collectors, making dreary prospects of their very survival.

Practically murder.

And, when she came across a copy of *Song Of The Cardinal* by Gene Stratton-Porter, that had been beautifully rebound and was not missing a single page, she simply snapped. Unlike her own at home that was dog-eared and missing three, this wonderful book she had always made required reading in her high school literature class (way back in her teaching days) was probably headed for some trash bin. That being the case, what could be wrong with making an exchange?

So, she did.

After that, she found a perfect copy of *Mama's Way* by Thyra Ferré Bjorn, a slender little volume that no overworked, underpaid wife and mother should be deprived of referring to during hard times. The secrets held between those covers were priceless. Stella already owned two copies of it herself (one for keeps and one for loaning) so she simply re-shelved the little jewel in its appropriate place and removed its information from the discard file.

That was the beginning of her "Save the Good Literature Campaign."

Before she knew it, there were stacks of

these marvels from every subject and decade since the Revolution. Stella became a walking Bill of Rights for books, and she felt as if she hadn't done anything so important in her entire life. Which was why —when the problems arose—she was forced to take such drastic measures.

How on earth was she going to remove nearly a hundred books from the discard room when she had to walk right under Ms. Thatcher's nose to do it? It was one thing to secret one or two small books inside one's clothing on the way to the ladies' room and then make a detour for re-shelving, but there simply wasn't enough time left for that. As Ms. Thatcher explained, the discard work took little more than two weeks every year to accomplish and that in time for the "all community" sale just before Christmas.

Sponsored by the Friends of the Library.

But where there's a will, there's a way. Stella had always possessed a talent for being resourceful and engaging when she needed to be. So, she devised a plan based on the age-old admonition that "a gift will make a way for you." It would take money out of her moving fund, but what great cause wasn't worth some personal loss to accomplish? The trouble was she had no idea she had so much to lose. And (in her state of mind) the plan seemed nothing short of harmless genius.

It took most of one paycheck and all of her next day off to prepare. Along with an Old World recipe for wassail, a crock pot, and two quarts of spirits. The fact that Stella was not a drinker, and hundred-year-old recipes tend to lose things in translation, she made her first mistake by assuming that the word "spirits" meant a mixture of everything. So, into the pot went two cups each of brandy, gin, whiskey, and the most potent of Jamaican rums.

Considering that just tasting the brew during its various stages sent her to bed early for the best night's sleep she had experienced in years. (She should have thought twice about the size of her gift bottle. Only she didn't.) She filled a large Mason jar to the brim, decorated the cap with a festive piece of gift-wrap and holly, and wrote: "To Ms. Thatcher—tidings of comfort and joy" on the tag.

The following day, when bringing the usual afternoon coffee into the supervisor's office before taking her own and disappearing into the little discard room, Stella placed her "gift" on the desk beside it.

"What's this?" asked Ms. Thatcher.

"Oh, just an old family recipe I like to share during the holidays. Starting off on the wrong foot the way I have with everybody, I sort of wanted to make amends."

"Why, thank you, Stella. That's very thoughtful."

"Gave some to that Colonel Henry, too," she confided, "and left some in the lounge for our staff party, this afternoon."

"I'm sure everyone will enjoy it. And the Colonel's turned into such a fixture around here we always invite him to the staff parties. Never stays though."

"No?"

"No. Just comes in long enough to review the troops—as he says—and wish everyone Merry Christmas. How are the discards coming?"

"Oh—fine. Fine. Almost finished."

"Good. The volunteers will be by on Monday to pick them up. Big event, that community sale. Takes days to set up."

"I'll bet."

The staff party was scheduled for four-thirty. Even if Ms. Thatcher didn't taste her "gift" or leave her desk until then, she would at least head for the lounge at that time. That would give Stella plenty of time to wheel her book cart through the office and back into the stacks for re-shelving. With the early closing, and the staff pre-occupied, she felt sure she could accomplish her mission.

Of course, it wasn't a permanent solution. But considering no one had caught the shelving error of *The Egg And 1* for over fifteen years, Stella felt fairly certain that many of her "special placements" would be safe (yet available) for many years to come. Mostly because she had purposely misplaced them randomly in the database, so that even a Clerk I person would return them to the wrong spot.

Providence seemed to be with her.

Instead of the long wait she expected, Ms. Thatcher must have been suddenly called away from her desk, and Stella was able to wheel the book cart through dangerous territory at quarter past three. More providence! She set the printer to run off ten copies of the discard list so noise would continue to be heard from her little work area, and set out on her quest.

It was short-lived. Twenty minutes into the project, she was interrupted by an urgent, "Psssssst!" at the end of the isle. It was the Colonel. He was red- faced and huffing, with a lock of that wavy gray hair fallen onto his forehead, as if he had been running frantically through the stacks like a billiard ball caught in a pinball machine.

"Good grief, woman!" he whispered emphatically, "What have you done? They're calling the police!"

"What?" It didn't seem logical that anyone could accuse her of stealing when she hadn't actually removed any of the books from the building. Other than that one copy of...

"Ms. Thatcher just dropped over dead! They say you poisoned her!"

4

"Oh, dear!" Stella felt faint and the room began to sway.

"Steady, girl—steady!" He braced her under an elbow and propelled her toward the nearest overstuffed chair at the end of the isle. "I haven't tasted anything with a kick like that since my old Army days. Surely you knew about Ms. Thatcher's condition?"

"Oh, dear!" she wailed, again. "I'm going to be sick...I'm going to faint!"

"Are you a praying woman?"

"I don't know what to pray!" Stella felt a big lump of panic coming into her throat.

"God help me. I wouldn't hurt anyone if you paid me!"

"Just what I thought. We'll go with that, then."

"Are they going to arrest me? Oh, God help me!" And thus began a rather strange partnership that Stella would always be grateful for. Whether it was the fierce potency of her Old World Wassail, the Colonel's chivalrous impulse to help a lady in distress, or a truly divine intervention, she never knew.

At any rate, the impressive stature of Colonel Oliver P. Henry (he was not dressed in Hawaiian that day, but rather a pressed shirt and tie: probably in anticipation of reviewing the troops), whose subsequent demands that unless they could come up with more proof, Stella should be allowed to go home. He even agreed to take full responsibility for her. Such steadfastness was the only thing that kept her from falling to pieces entirely and having to be removed to the nearest looney bin.

Because in that one brief but horrible instance, her whole life as she knew it was at stake... and not even the children of the future seemed worth giving it all up for. Selfish but true. One hardly feels like a saint while being accused of murder.

There was definitely an accusation of murder.

In fact—according to Ester Fergussen—Ms. Thatcher had been poisoned. By none other than Stella Madison, whom everyone knew hadn't been able to get along with a single member of the staff since she arrived. Especially Ms. Thatcher. Something about a crazy sort of affectation over books, and their beloved supervisor being personally responsible for poisoning the minds of children. Why—Ester went on while one of the officers was taking it all down—Stella was always talking about poison in one way or another.

Mr. Bruce from the research department even agreed with her.

Not that it was typical for police officers to believe every accusation people made under such circumstances. It was the glaring fact that Ms. Thatcher was found still clutching a broken piece of the Mason jar Stella had given her, and she fairly reeked with the brew. Considering it could take nearly a week for lab and autopsy reports to come back that might prove otherwise...

It didn't look good for Stella.

Looking back on it all later, she was shocked at how one minute things could be going along in a normal fashion, and then—boom! Out of nowhere some horrible catastrophe that could have ruined the rest of her entire life suddenly had a stranglehold on her. To go to jail at her age, when she had never even gone to traffic court would have been the death of Stella Madison. As it was, it was only the Colonel's sheer strength of character and quick thinking that pulled her through. And after the way she had treated him, too! No one had ever gone out of their way like that for her before.

Yet, there he was, practically a stranger, standing up for her as if they were the dearest of friends. She didn't even have to go down to the police station after she gave them all of her personal information. Which would have been quite beyond her, she was sure of it. After ten years of utter seclusion, living in a world where her closest human contact was her doctor, even the thought of being thrown in with the kind of criminals one saw on TV, was terrifying.

And to make matters worse, it was nearly eight o'clock by the time they were all allowed to finally leave the library (except poor Ms. Thatcher, who had been taken away earlier in an ambulance)... and it was already dark. On top of everything else, she was going to have to walk home through dark city streets all by herself. Her absolute worst fear. Something she vowed she would never be stupid enough to do. Stella could almost feel her knees turning to jelly, again, as she stood beneath the amber light of the nearest streetlamp in the parking lot and watched, in horror, as everyone else disappeared.

Except for the Colonel, still standing beside her. "Where's your car?"

"I'm afraid I... I don't have one."

"Better let me drive you, then."

Saved, again.

By the time he helped her with her key (her hands were shaking too much to get it into the lock), Stella felt as if she might collapse before she even made it to the couch. But the soothing strains of a Christmas CD she had left on, the twinkling lights on her tree, and the mouth-watering aroma of Irish stew simmering in the crock pot, all converged at once to help calm her nerves.

"You'll feel better now that you're home," the colonel offered, still standing at the door as if he were afraid of barging in. "Would you like me to turn on your tea water before I go, Stella?"

Stella burst into tears. Aftershock, no doubt, but embarrassing, none the less. All formalities aside, the Colonel was beside her in an instant. Not that he interrupted. He simply took the burgundy colored afghan from the back of the couch, tucked it in all around her, patted her on the shoulder as one would a child, and let her cry things out. By the time it was over, there was a steaming cup of tea and bowl of stew on the coffee table in front of her. After that, he handed her his own handkerchief, and she blew her nose just as the words of the old Finnish carol wafted out over her like a benediction...

"Good King Wenceslas looked out
On the feast of Stephen
When the snow lay round about
Deep and crisp and even..."

In that moment, the Colonel—eyes lit with friendly concern and his cheeks flushed with a pleasant warmth of central heating she had left turned up to eighty—seemed like nothing less than the benevolent king, himself. Standing there, in person, in her own living room. "I don't know how to thank you enough, Colonel Henry," she sniffed.

"Call me, Oliver."

"Oliver. I think I'll be all right, now. I wouldn't want to keep you from your family any longer. They're probably wondering what on earth..."

"My dear, I'm an old bachelor. The only thing waiting for me back home is half an enchilada from last night's take-out dinner I was going to warm up in the microwave."

"Well, for heaven sake—would you like a bowl of stew?"

"Love one. I admit I had a taste dishing yours up, and it's delicious."

So it was that they had their first meal together, sitting in a companionable silence, and letting the terrible strains of the strange day melt away like an outside chill. Neither made small talk, or put on airs. Stella barely managed to finish half of hers, while the Colonel dished himself another bowl.

"What do you think will happen to me, now?" Stella finally ventured as she sipped on her tea.

"You don't know how lucky you are to be home instead of in the klinker, tonight."

"Oh, but I do. It was like a miracle—an out-and- out miracle."

"You must have angels watching out for you."

"Is that what you are?"

"Who, me? Not even close." Then he laughed at the thought. A pleasant rolling laugh that came bubbling out like a pot boiling over.

"But why did you help me?"

He didn't answer right away, but sat for a moment with his bottom lip stuck out in thought, as if carefully weighing what he was about to say. Finally, "I helped you because I knew you were innocent. Knew it in my gut, and it was the right thing to do. Couldn't have lived with myself otherwise.

Besides," he said, getting up and carrying their bowls to the sink, "anyone who reacts the way you did about young Johnson coming home, can't be half bad."

"I don't know."

"Well, I do. I write about young heroes. They're my specialty. I'm a pretty good judge of character, too. Even if I do say so, myself. Do my eyes deceive me, or is that really a pumpkin pie I see in this refrigerator?"

"Help yourself," said Stella. "Whipped cream is in that little blue bowl right next to it."

"You mean fresh-whipped cream?"

"Cooking is one of my weaknesses. I'll probably have to work my way through my entire holiday cookbook just to keep from going crazy waiting for the coroner's report on poor Ms. Thatcher!"

"I think I can help you with that."

The entire ordeal—which was to last almost till Christmas– left Stella not only shaken and humiliated, but quite depleted of even a trace of energy she might have left in her for any more causes. However lofty they might be. What's more, she was seriously worried if she could keep herself out of any similar scrapes if she took another job. Not if she couldn't even see them coming. Because it had become very clear to her that even the strictest and most well-meaning people could get caught out in the dark sometimes.

There were simply no guarantees in

life.

Still, here she was, enjoying what might be called an amazing reprieve from a narrowly avoided disaster, sharing a quiet dinner of celebration. She and Colonel Henry were seated at the table nearest the giant tropical fish tank in the Luau Palace, on the day the coroner's report finally came through. It declared that Ms. Thatcher had died of heart failure brought on by years of chronic heart disease that had never been attended to. She hadn't even tasted Stella's wassail. It had only shattered and spilled all over her when she fell to the floor.

With the whole ugly business behind her, now, Stella could finally get serious about finding that new place to live. But with barely a week left to go, she had better quit being so picky.

"Any luck today?" the Colonel asked, as if he had read her mind.

"One that might come available after New Year's, but that doesn't exactly help me now."

"You ought to come over to my complex. It isn't anything like you're used to, but there's a vacancy two doors down."

"I probably couldn't afford it," she sighed.

"Anyone could afford it. It's just a big rambling old mansion that used to be owned by some Hollywood director during the thirties. Been turned into a ramshackle of apartments, now, but what it lacks in privacy, it makes up in charm."

"You mean, it's just rooms for rent, without kitchens or private bathrooms?"

"Oh, you get several rooms. Each one with a bath and kitchenette. It's just that you have to walk through the main house to get in. And the people who live there are one of the oddest assortment of misfits I've ever known. It's why I spend so much time at the library. But it could at least be a temporary place until you found something better."

"You might get very tired of me as a neighbor," she warned. "Don't you think

I've caused you enough trouble, already?"

"No trouble at all. In fact, I haven't had so much excitement in years. And you were right about all the good books, you know. Right from the very beginning." He drummed his fingers on the table and looked over the menu. "I think I'll go for the Mandarin duck, this time."

"But I never even got to finish carrying out my plan."

"Nonsense. Your plan worked! The next Clerk I that came in put the rest of the books away safely without so much as a thought they might not be cataloged properly. I checked, myself, the day after they fired you."

"You did? What a nice thing!" He really was quite the wonderful person. Stella had never known anyone like him.

"It's just like you said, Stella." he went on. "Hardly any thinking at all going on anymore. Remarkable of you to actually do something about it. Not many people will step up and take a hand in things, you know."

"I really don't understand what came over me," she admitted.

He refilled their little bowls of tea from the steaming teapot on their table. "I do wish you'd take that vacancy, Stella. Especially since you're not working at the library any more. I don't mind saying I'd feel a lot better if you were somewhere I could keep an eye out for you."

"You know, Oliver," she reminded him, "I did manage to take fairly decent care of myself before you ever came along."

"Oh, quite. Quite. Didn't mean to imply that. I suppose it's me that would be better off if you were close by. That's the real truth of it."

The real truth was, that Stella had not managed to take care of herself as decently as she thought she had all this time. And she had certainly been headed for disaster if the Colonel hadn't miraculously been there to ward it off. But why go into all that.

Except...

"I'd like that, too," she finally replied. "But I can't guarantee trouble won't follow me right on over there, Oliver. Trouble just seems sneak up behind me when I least expect it."

"Hmpf! Trouble's after everybody. But we're praying people, aren't we. You might say we have a guarantee. It's what we praying people get for being on God's side. He watches our backs to make sure nothing gets us from behind."

"You make it sound like we're all in some sort of war," Stella looked over the menu with the delicious sensation of trying to decide between sweet-and-sour or teriyaki, without the guilty twinge of having to count pennies.

"Of course we are! The war between good and evil. Been going on since the beginning of time. Why don't you go for half of each, they don't mind doing that, here."

"Wouldn't that be wonderful if it were

true."

"Of course, it's true. But I'll ask the waiter if you want me to make sure."

"Not the half-and-half. God protecting you from things you aren't even aware of."

"He does if you ask him to."

"But I haven't asked him anything for years. I can't even remember the last time I prayed." There, she said it. It had come right out just as easily as if she had meant to all along, and it hadn't been hard, after all. With the Colonel thinking so highly of her, she wanted to be perfectly honest. And she certainly didn't want to be masquerading as something she wasn't. Especially after all these years of actually blaming God for having to live alone and take care of herself for so long.

"I distinctly remember you asking him to help you, not once, but twice, during the catastrophe," he reminded her. "And I'll bet my bottom dollar you meant every word."

"But that was nothing but...but sheer

desperation!"

"That's all it takes, Stella."

"Are you sure?"

"Call upon me in the day of trouble and I will save you... Psalm 50:15, as I recall."

"But what if you don't deserve it?"

"Nobody deserves it. That's the point. The only way you can miss out on it is if you never ask."

Stella couldn't have been more stunned if someone had told her she just won the lottery. But how could she be sure it was true? Then it flashed through her mind what might have happened if Oliver hadn't been there to stand up for her, and they had taken her off to jail. She wouldn't have been able to survive it. Even if they acquitted her, she might have ended up in some mental institution. A prisoner of circumstance and her own tormenting fears. But nothing like that had happened.

Colonel Oliver P. Henry had shown up and been kind to her, even after she had been so insulting to him. He had stood by her every step of the way. What's more, on top of everything else, she was enjoying the best holiday season she had in years, because she was not sitting in her apartment all alone. Why... since she had said those few simple words... her whole life had turned around!

If she were to look at it that way.

Of course, a person could explain it all by looking at things logically. But that didn't change the fact of how different things were before she "prayed" than how they were after. Not to mention that she was happy. Why, she was almost giddy with the amount of happiness she had felt over the last few days. It was as if last week her life had been meant to end in horrors, but she had literally been snatched out of that disaster and set lovingly in an even better place than she had been rescued from. And just in time, too.

Home before dark, after all.

Author's Note

John Newton (whose words were quoted at the beginning of this story) went to sea at the age of eleven and became involved in the slave trade. Through many hardships, and several years where he himself was a slave in West Africa, he was finally rescued by a sea captain whom his father had sent to look for him. On the way home, the ship encountered a storm off the coast and started to sink. It was the middle of the night. Newton called out to God as it filled up with water, and right afterward, some floating cargo stopped up the hole and they were able to drift safely to land.

Not only did John Newton leave the slave trade and become a clergyman, he eventually wrote a pamphlet that was instrumental in influencing the Slave Trade Act of 1807 that abolished the slave trade in the British Empire. He is also the author of the popular hymn, _Amazing Grace_.

About Lilly Maytree...

Lilly Maytree is the author of *Gold Trap, The Pandora Box*, and *The Stella Madison Capers*. Books that sent her careening along on her "Mystery Tours" with her captain husband aboard the *Glory B.* She loves sharing these adventures with readers. It has even been said that she time-travels (but that's probably just a rumor). To find out about her current adventures, simply visit:

LillyMaytree.com

You can get in touch with her via the contact page. It might take a few days if she is adventuring far away... but she always comes back sooner or later.

Other Books By
Lilly Maytree

The Stella Madison Capers...

Home Before Dark
(Caper #1)

Here is the first of the Stella Madison Capers, the story of how everything started, and how she escaped from a catastrophe that seemed to come out of nowhere. Which is the nature of catastrophes but it's so hard to be logical when you're in the middle of one. It's also the story of how she met the colonel (if you're interested in that sort of thing).

A Thief in the House
(Caper #2)

Stella Madison is back, this time with a bevy of friends. But just how far should a person go when it comes to sticking by their friends? There's a thief in the rambling old mansion she moved into. And while it was someone who was quick to lend help when Stella needed it most, how can she possibly return the favor without jeopardizing herself along with them? No person is obligated to go that far... right?

Collections...

Voyage of the Dreadnaught

collection of 4 Stella Madison Capers

Here is a collection of the four Stella Madison Capers covering the entire voyage of the Dreadnaught, through the Inside Passage to Alaska. Includes: **Sea Trials, The Pushover Plot, Lost in the Wilderness**, and **The Last Resort.** Also includes a brief account of Lilly Maytree's true-life voyage along the same route, in the sailboat, *Glory B.*

Novels...

Gold Trap

Megan Jennings is headed to Africa for high adventure and divine appointments until she makes a small wrong turn. But what is faith, if not to strike out against impossible odds believing you will win? Or leap out into the dark knowing someone will be there to catch you? Someone does catch her... but it isn't who she was expecting.

The Pandora Box
Journalist D.J. Parker learns the location of a famous cache of diamonds that were stolen during World War II. What she doesn't know is—the federal government has been following the case for years. With an old journal to lead the way, she sets out aboard a yacht that once carried the infamous Herman Goering. A thrilling treasure hunt that could either prove to be the adventure of a lifetime... or her worst nightmare.

For Writers...

Unspoken Rules

Popular books (those stories everyone likes no matter what the subject) all have certain things in common. And what they have most in common is what they DON'T do. Within the following pages, dear writer, you will find the three most important "don'ts" of popular fiction that I learned when I was studying the masters. Why? Because I love research and I never mind sharing my notes.

Writing Rules!

(a mysterious student handbook)

A mysterious little desktop handbook that can help anyone (well, almost anyone) with writing rules. Especially if you are a student and have to write things all the time.

For Parents...

Behave Yourself!

Teaching your children to discipline themselves.

Are you tired of bickering during daily routines encroaching on way too much of your family time? Here is a book that offers a two-week program that teaches your children to discipline themselves. Hard to believe? Here are the step-by-step secrets of how it's done, and why it works.

The Nature of Children
(And how to deal with it.)

A manual based on a compilation of parenting articles Lilly wrote over several years as a columnist for Childcare Magazine. It is a result of many requests from parents for more information about that content and the foundation of the methods she used both in raising her own children, and in her classrooms.

After years of experience, she has a lot to say about what motivates children and has implemented many of her unique ideas into books and programs that others can use.

An excerpt from
Stella Madison Caper #2...

A Thief In The House
A Stella Madison Caper

by Lilly Maytree

1

Stella Madison felt as if she had walked into a fortune. Considering her new apartment cost less than half what her other one did (and had nearly twice the space), there was even enough left over in her budget to loosen her belt a little. After all these years! For the first few weeks she was in heaven. To be honest, it wasn't really what one would call an apartment, but to Stella, it was even better.

It had charm – Old World charm – and if there was anything she loved more than books, it was places that even remotely resembled days gone by. True, the "Villa" had definitely seen better days. A rambling old mansion overlooking southern California's sea in one of the city's oldest sections. Even in this economy, the place would cost millions if put on the market, in spite of the fact it hadn't been properly cared for in years.

The landlady was a likeable, middle-aged widow named, Millie, who sported a bountiful figure and a head of thick auburn hair without a speck of gray in it. Always done up in a rather sixties-fashion French twist. Stella felt an immediate kinship with Millie. While her ramshackle renovations had turned the once-stately mansion into a hodge-podge of individual living quarters, each had its own unique flavor.

It was hard choosing between the third floor rooms with a balcony but no outside entrance, or, the ground level suite next to the main kitchen that had French doors which led right out into a garden. In the end she picked the upstairs because of the delicious quiet, and that adorable private balcony she could enjoy in her pajamas (if she had a mind to) and watch the many moods of the distant sea.

Besides that, the Colonel was only two doors away.

His set of rooms occupied the same floor on the south end and included a converted attic that made for vaulted ceilings and slanted windows. Two of which opened onto to the roof. Out there he had placed a patio table with chairs, and innumerable clay pots full of all manner of growing things. It was obvious that this was mostly where his incredible tan came from. One could see the swimming pool from there, along with a Greek statue (some woman named Phoebe with one arm broken off and the other holding a pitcher), but there had been no water in the pool for years. Too much work to maintain, Millie said, though when her husband was alive there were parties nearly every weekend during the summer. Movie people drove all the way up from Hollywood just to escape the sweltering heat.

Now parties of any kind were rare, and the Villa's "guests" consisted mostly of a few regular tenants. Each possessed some oddity that had endeared them to Millie, and none of them were wealthy. Counting Stella and the Colonel, there were six, along with three others who dropped by for meals. There was a retired carpenter, a bank teller, a teacher (some cousin of Millie's who had retired early on disability), and even a senator. Stella later discovered the senator to be only eight months old and the illegitimate son of the bank teller, who felt he might fare better in life with a more respectable name.

In coming to the Villa, Stella hadn't just moved into a new home but a new family. Something she hadn't had in years. A rather odd one, to be sure, but a type of family nevertheless. With all her new-found friends to help out, the dreaded task of moving actually turned into somewhat of an adventure. Which is why when the second crisis struck it didn't send her into as much of an emotional loop as the first one had. Thank heaven. Because that sort of stress isn't good for anyone, much less a woman in her sixties.

It happened on a Thursday.

While Stella was staring intently into her bathroom mirror, carefully applying a thin line of schoolroom glue to her upper lip before pressing on a false white mustache. Suddenly, a blood-curdling scream that echoed all the way up to her third floor apartment, stopped her cold before she could even get it on straight. For a moment she froze. What in the world? Without another thought, she flew out the door and down the two long flights of stairs, across the main foyer and along the hall, through the dining room and into the large kitchen. An exertion which completely winded her.

To read the rest of this Stella Madison
Caper, visit us online at:
LightsmithPublishers.com

Thank you for reading this book! Will you consider writing a review for it at your favorite online bookstore? In the meantime, may you be specially blessed, knowing that you have blessed others simply by reading their stories.

If you enjoyed reading this Lightsmith Publishers story, please share it with someone. You can also find other inspirational stories by visiting:

LigtsmithPuhblishers.com

If you have children, you may even enjoy browsing the "mysteriously different books" over at:

SummersIslandPress.com

Both imprints are divisions of the Wilderness School Institute, a nonprofit educational organization based in Thorne Bay, Alaska, where they "take learning back to nature." You can find more information about them here:

WildernessSchoolInstitute.org